You Can't Catch Me!

by Brock Turner

illustrated by Brenda Cantell

Blake
EDUCATION
Better ways to learn

Lexile® measure: 330L
For more information visit: www.Lexile.com

You Can't Catch Me! ISBN 978 1 86509 363 5

Blake Education Pty Ltd
ACN 074 266 023
Locked Bag 2022
Glebe 2037
Ph (02) 8585 4085
Fax (02) 8585 4058
Email: info@blake.com.au
Website: www.blake.com.au

Text copyright © 2000 Brock Turner
Illustrations copyright © 2000 Blake Education
Illustrated by Brenda Cantell
Reprinted 2001, 2006, 2013, 2017
Lexile Copyright © 2013 MetaMetrics, Inc.

Series publisher: Katy Pike
Page layout: Artwork Express
Printed by 1010 Printing International Ltd

Jenny

Craig

Jenny Can't Run

At lunchtime everyone played
Chasings.

Jenny was always one of the first
to get caught.

Craig made fun of Jenny. He said she was a slow runner. He said she had snail legs. He said she'd never catch him.

After you were caught, you had to chase the others. Jenny spent a lot of time chasing the others.

CHAPTER 2

Craig Is a Show-off

Craig was a pretty fast runner. He was always one of the last to get caught. He was also a show-off, a big loudmouthed show-off.

"You can't catch me! You can't catch me!" chanted Craig. He stood just out of Jenny's reach.

Boy oh boy, this made Jenny angry. She ran at him. He dodged out of her way.

Craig stopped just out of Jenny's reach again.

The other kids stood and watched. They should have been helping Jenny catch Craig.

Jenny was fed up. She'd had enough.

In a big rush she said to Craig,
"I bet I can skip longer than you
can."

"No way," said Craig. "We're playing Chasings, not Skippings! And you can't catch me."

CHAPTER 3

Chicken

A few of the kids giggled. Jenny didn't like it. She felt like walking away.

She felt shy and her face went red. But then she saw the look on Craig's face. He knew he'd won again.

She couldn't let them all laugh at her. She looked at Craig and said, "I think you're chicken."

Then she made the "brrrkkk brrrkkk brrrkkk" noise that chickens make. Now the others were laughing at Craig.

She could see that he didn't like it.

"Good," she thought, "now he knows how it feels."

"I'm not chicken," said Craig. He turned to walk away.

Jenny made the chicken noises again.

"Brrrkkk, brrrkkk, brrrkkk. You're a scaredy-cat," she said to Craig.

Everyone laughed. A few kids started making chicken noises too.

"OK, OK," said Craig, "I'll skip. We start at the same time. The first one to stop loses."

"Sounds fair to me," said Jenny. She was a bit scared. She really wanted to win.

Skipping

Jenny got her skipping rope out of her bag. Craig borrowed one.

The playground was now packed with kids. Everyone wanted to see who would win.

Jenny didn't like everyone staring at her. Craig looked a bit nervous too.

Sally told them to get ready. She counted down, "3, 2, 1, GO!"

Jenny and Craig started to skip. Most of the school was there watching them.

CHAPTER 5

The Winner!

They skipped for a couple of minutes. Jenny was getting tired.

Jenny tried to slow down her skipping.

"Slower will be easier," she thought.

Then Jenny caught her foot in the rope. She almost tripped over. She started to think that Craig would win again.

Suddenly, there was a thump beside her. Craig had tripped over. She had won!

Jenny had thought she would feel great but she didn't. She felt a bit funny.

She looked down at Craig sitting on the ground. He had a bloody knee. The other kids were laughing at him.

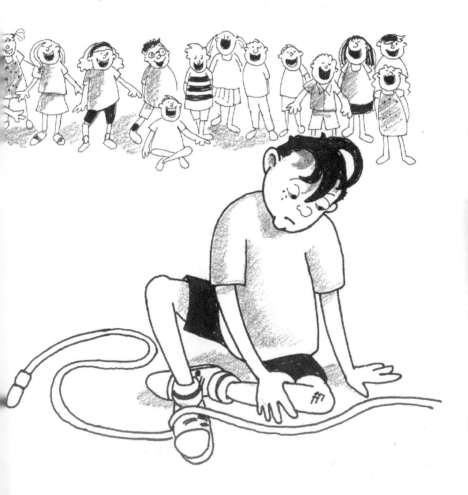

"Are you all right Craig?" Jenny
asked.

"Of course I'm OK," Craig grunted.

"Look," said Jenny, "you're a good
runner and I'm a good skipper."

"So what?" said Craig.

"Soooo ..." said Jenny, "you're not better than me and I'm not better than you. No more teasing, OK?"

Craig didn't say anything for a minute. Then he muttered, "OK."

The bell rang. It was time to line up to go back into class.

After school, Jenny ran to meet her mum.

"See you tomorrow Craig," she called.

"Yeah," he smiled and waved. "Bye."

 **GLOSSARY**

chanted
repeated in a
sing-song way

dodged
moved aside quickly

grunted
made a sound like a pig

loudmouth
someone who speaks too loudly

nervous
being scared

scaredy-cat
a coward

shy
very timid

tripped
stumbled

Brock Turner

How high can you jump?

Not very.

Why do ants have 6 legs?

The same reason that dogs have 4 and spiders have 8.

What is your favourite toy?

My computer now, but definitely my bike when I was younger.

What is the hardest part of your day?

Waking up in the morning.

When did you write your first book?

When I was 15 I wrote for the school magazine.

Who was your hero as a child?

My parents because they were the greatest people around and the 6 million dollar man because he was invincible.

Brenda Cantell

How high can you jump?

Depends how big the crab is.

Why do ants have 6 legs?

So they can swim through honey.

What is your favourite toy?

My puppy even though he's only made of Dacron.

What is the hardest part of your day?

Doing the dishes.

When did you draw your first picture?

When I was five I drew our budgie. For the first time one of my drawings looked real.

Who was your hero as a child?

My aunty who went away and travelled the world in a boat.

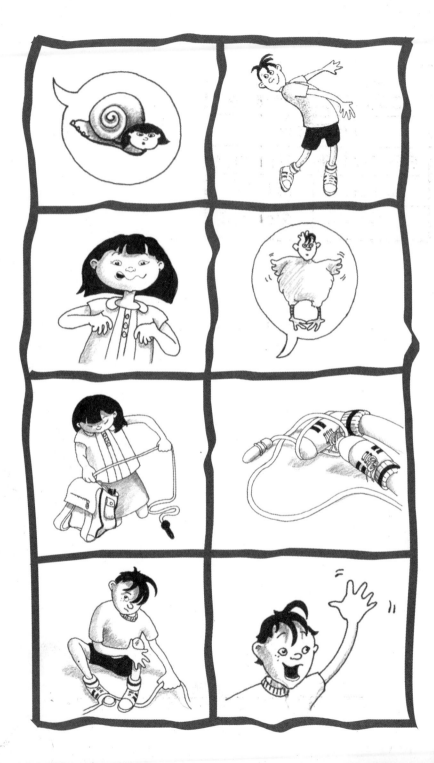